LOVE, ALWAYS

# MAD AT SCHOOL
## Kyky

## BY KATE MOORE

Published and written by Kate Moore

Illustrated by Sudesha Shrestha, Anamika Gautam

ISBN: 978-1-9995539-0-6

Copyright © 2018 by Kate Moore

To all my children

Love, always.

Kyky was excited. She knew it was almost time for school to be over because Clock looked like this.

Kyky liked school, but she liked time with Mama and Papa more. Today Mama and Papa were picking her up together. Mama would kiss her cheek. Papa would give her a monster hug. There would be lots of Love, always.

That's what they said before they went to sleep.

Kyky would shout from her bed, "Love?"

And Mama and Papa would answer, "Always!"

Kindergarten was usually fun, but not yesterday.

Yesterday Robbie punched her in the the arm when she accidentally broke his midnight blue crayon.

She made a mean face and punched him back.

When Mama came to pick her up, Mrs

Bingham told her what happened.

Mama said, "Kyky. Love, always."

Today Robbie tore the corner of Kyky's

rainbow painting on purpose.


Kyky wanted to punch him again.

Robbie glared at Kyky. Kyky glared at Robbie.

Her punching fist was ready, and she saw that
Robbie's punching fist was ready too.

Then Kyky closed her eyes

and whispered to herself,

"Love, always."

*Ahhhhh...*

Kyky's punching fist went away,

and she put some tape on her rainbow.

*BRRRRRRRRNNGGGG!*

The bell meant it was time to leave!

All the girls and boys lined up.

Robbie was standing just in front of Kyky.

Mrs. Bingham smiled and waved as they all left the room.

At the big door that led outside, Robbie

stopped. He looked back at Kyky.

Then he held the door open wide for her!

Robbie looked at Kyky.

Kyky looked at Robbie.

They both smiled.

Kyky ran over to Mama and Papa. Mama kissed her on her cheek. Papa gave her a monster hug.

They walked home together.

Love, always.

Made in the USA
Monee, IL
11 January 2020

20182061R00019